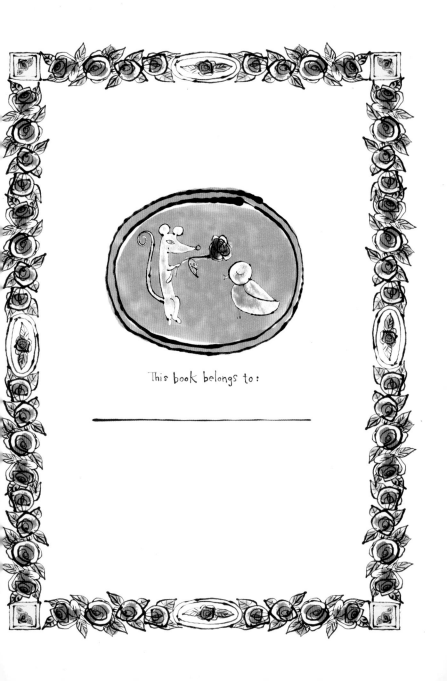

This book belongs to:

_____

The English Roses

by

MADONNA

Illustrated By

Jeffrey Fulvimari

CALLAWAY
NEW YORK
2006

For Lola and Rocco

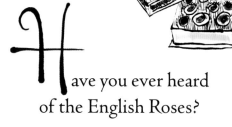

H

ave you ever heard
of the English Roses?

Here is what they are not:
A box of chocolates.
A football team.
Flowers growing in the garden.

What they are is this:
Four little girls named
Nicole, Amy, Charlotte, and Grace.

The english Roses

We're
#1

Nicole   Amy   Charlotte   Grace

Here are some things you should know about them:
They go to the same school and live in the same
neighborhood. They play the same games,
read the same books, and like the same boys.

They have picnics in the summer and ice-skating
parties in the winter. They are practically glued
to each other at the hip.

Most of all, they love to dance. . . .

techno
Fox-trot

(vogue)

the
tickety
boo

It all sounds so perfectly fun and nice.
And in many ways, it was. But there was only
one problem. They were all a little bit jealous
of another girl in the neighborhood.

Her name was Binah, and here are
some things you should know about her:
She was very, very beautiful.
She had long, silky hair and skin like milk and honey.
She was an excellent student and very good at sports.
She was always kind to people.
She was special.

But she was sad. Because even though she was
the most beautiful girl anyone had ever seen,
she was also very lonely. She had no friends,
and everywhere she went, she was alone.

By now, you are probably wondering, "What's the big deal? If she was so nice, why didn't the English Roses invite her over for a cup of tea?"

Listen, I already told you why. Because they were a little jealous. Well, maybe more than a little. Haven't you ever been green with envy? Or felt like you were about to explode if you didn't get what somebody else had? If you say no, you are telling a big, fat fib, and I am going to tell your mother.

Now, stop interrupting me.

*Y*ou see, the English Roses wanted to be friendly, and they knew that Binah was lonely. But they could not bring themselves to be nice to her, because everywhere they went, this is what they heard:

"What a beauty she is!"

"She shines like a star!"

"That Binah is something else!"

When Nicole and Amy and Charlotte and Grace heard people speak this way about Binah, they always felt like they were going to be sick. This is what they would say:

"How could anyone be so perfect?"

"No one ever says that about us!"

"It's not fair to have so much!"

"Let's pretend we don't see her when she walks by."

"Let's push her into the lake!"

And that is what they did.

No, silly, not the lake part, the pretending not to see her part.

And so time went on, and the English Roses continued to have fun with each other, while Binah remained alone.

*O*ne night, when all the girls were having
a sleepover party at Nicole's house, her mother
peeked her head around the corner and said,
"Do you mind if I come in and have a chat
with all of you?"

"Don't worry, Mum, we're going to go to bed soon,"
said Nicole. "Just let us finish our pillow fight!"

"That's not why I came in here," her mother replied.
"I want to talk to you about Binah. She lives down
the street, she goes to your school, she likes to do
all the same things you like to do, and yet you never
invite her over or make any effort to be friendly
with her."

There was a very long pause.

The English Roses looked around the room at one another. Amy was the first to speak. "She thinks she's God's gift to creation just because she's beautiful."

"Yes, why should we invite her over? She gets enough attention already," Charlotte joined in.

"It's not that we don't like her," said Nicole. "It's just that she's probably stuck up. Pretty girls usually are."

Nicole's mother thought about this for a moment, and then she said, "I think you girls are being unfair. She looks like she could really use a friend, and you haven't even had a conversation with her. How do you know what kind of a person she is? How would you like it if people decided whether they were going to be nice to you based on how you look?"

The girls knew she had a point, but they didn't want to say it. Suddenly, they didn't feel like having a pillow fight.

"Please think about what I've said," said Nicole's mother, and she stood up and kissed them all good night.

When her mother was gone, Nicole turned out the light, and the girls lay awake in the dark for quite a while thinking about what Nicole's mother had said. No one said a word, and eventually they all fell fast asleep.

And while they were sleeping, they each had the same dream.

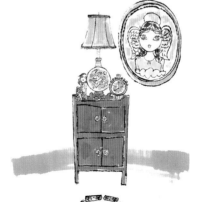

Here is what they dreamed:
All four of them were having a picnic
in the park, complaining (as usual) about how
beautiful Binah was, how she got tooooooooo
much attention, and how unfair it was for them,
when suddenly, a fairy godmother appeared!
She was short and plump and very jolly looking.

Listen, why am I telling you this? Don't you
know what a fairy godmother looks like?

Anyway, she landed right on top of Charlotte's
sandwich. "Oh, excuse me. Is that pumpernickel
bread?" she said, sniffing the air. "I just love
the smell of pumpernickel!"

he girls sat and stared at her with their mouths open, because they had never seen a fairy godmother before. "Ahem," said the fairy godmother, clearing her throat, "Now, where was I? Oh yes, I couldn't help but overhear your conversation, and it sounds like you are all quite dissatisfied with who you are, which makes me very unhappy, and I would like to offer you the opportunity to be someone else."

"What do you mean?" asked Charlotte, pulling her sandwich out from underneath the fairy godmother's bottom.

"What I mean," replied the fairy, "and please do not interrupt me, is that, if you are so jealous of Binah, then by all means, you should be someone else. In fact, perhaps one of you would even like to trade places with Binah."

"Oh, that's silly. How could we possibly be someone else?" interrupted Grace.

"Well, if you would just let me finish," harrumphed the fairy, "when I sprinkle my magic dust over you, you can be whoever you'd like to be. But first, you might want to fly over to Binah's house with me and spend some time with her. Just to make sure that her life is to your liking. Or anyone else's for that matter."

The girls all gulped and nodded, and finally Nicole said, "But . . . but . . . she'll see us looking through the window, and she'll think we're burglars or something."

"Yes, she might call the police," added Amy.

"Oh, nonsense," scoffed the fairy, nibbling on Charlotte's chocolate chip cookie. "When I sprinkle you with magic fairy dust,

you will be invisible, and you can go wherever
you want to go, and no one will ever see you."

The girls just sat there speechless, which didn't happen
very often, I can assure you.

"Well, don't just sit there stuffing your faces," tutted the fairy,
stuffing her face. "My time is very valuable."

The girls leaned forward and whispered quietly for a moment.
They decided that even though the fairy took their cookies
without asking, she seemed rather harmless, and anyway,
they couldn't turn down the chance to spy on Binah without
her knowing they were there.

So they asked to be sprinkled with fairy dust,
and off they flew to Binah's house.

Suddenly they found themselves sitting around Binah's kitchen table. And there, on her hands and knees, was Binah, scrubbing the floor. Sweat was dripping from her forehead, and she looked very tired.

All at once, her father came into the room and said, "It's getting late, Binah. When you've finished scrubbing the floor, I think you should start cooking dinner. I'm going outside to fix the car."

Binah smiled and said, "Okay, Papa."

Then he was gone.

$\mathcal{B}$inah proceeded to do a multitude of tasks. When she finished cleaning the floor . . .

she peeled potatoes . . .

she chopped onions . . .

she set the table . . .

she washed . . .

she scaled the fish . . .

and ironed the clothes . .

and finally,
she emptied the trash.

The English Roses couldn't believe their eyes.
They had never seen a girl work so hard in their lives.
"She reminds me of Cinderella," said Amy.

"She looks like she hasn't combed her hair
in a week," remarked Charlotte.

"Where is her mother?" asked Nicole.

"She doesn't have a mother," replied
the fairy godmother. "She lives alone with
her father, and he works all day, so when she
comes home from school, she has to clean the
house and wash the clothes and cook the dinner."

"**Y**ou mean, she does it all by herself?" asked Grace.

"Yes, you ninnies," answered the fairy. "I just said she lives alone with her father."

"Well, what happened to her mother?" asked Nicole.

"She died a very long time ago. Poor thing," sighed the fairy. "And as you know, Binah has no friends, so she spends all her time on her own.

"Well, come along then, girls. Would you like to see what her bedroom looks like?"

The English Roses all stood up to go, but they felt bad about leaving Binah behind all by herself with so much work.

"Oh, don't dawdle, ladies. I've got places to go and people to meet," said the fairy impatiently.

 So off they went to see if Binah's room was to their liking.

They were not prepared for what they saw:
A simple room with a single bed.
A chest of drawers. A shelf full of books.
There was, of course, one doll.
But only one. Can you believe it?
Well, you'd better, because I'm telling you.

There was one picture in a frame on the bedside table, and all the girls gathered around it to see who was in the picture. It was a beautiful photograph of Binah's mother. Nicole's eyes began to fill with tears. "I feel so bad," she said.

"It must be awful not to have a mother. She must feel terribly lonely," said Charlotte. "And we haven't been very nice to her."

"Well, what do you say?" interrupted the fairy godmother. "Anyone want to trade places?"

There was a very long pause.

The English Roses looked at one another.
It was so quiet, you could hear a pin drop.
"I think we've made a terrible mistake," said Grace.
"I can't imagine living without my mum."

"I don't want to do so many chores," said Amy.
"And I don't know the first thing about cooking."

"Well, is there anyone else you'd like to be?"
asked the fairy godmother. "Perhaps in another
neighborhood? Another city? Or even another
country? I'm sure I could arrange it for you."

"Please, just let us go home to our own cozy beds
and our families, whom we love," begged Nicole.

"Yes, we want to go home," cried the rest of the girls.

"Suit yourself," said the fairy. "But in the future,
you might think twice before grumbling that
someone else has a better life than you.
As I said before, I'm a very busy woman!"

In the blink of an eye, the English Roses were back
in bed, fast asleep.

When morning came, the girls awoke,
relieved to find that they were still
themselves. They told one another about their
dream, and they promised each other that,
from that day on, they would be kinder to Binah
and stop complaining about their own lives.

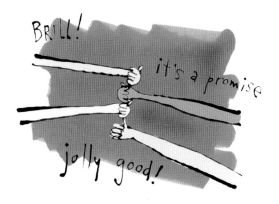

First they invited Binah to a tea party, and then they started walking to school with her, and not long after that, they were doing homework together. Binah even taught them how to bake an apple pie. They soon found out that she was very likable indeed.

They grew to love her like a sister and often went to her house to help her with her chores.

Time went by, and soon, everywhere the
English Roses went, Binah went with them.
And you're not going to believe this, but people
in the neighborhood started talking about them.

And this is what they said:
"Those English Roses are really special."
"What beautiful girls!"
"They'll grow up to be incredible women one day."

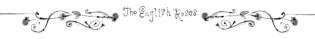

And you know what?
They did.

If you don't believe me,
then go and find out for yourself.
I didn't make this up.

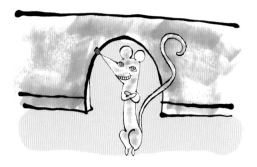

The End

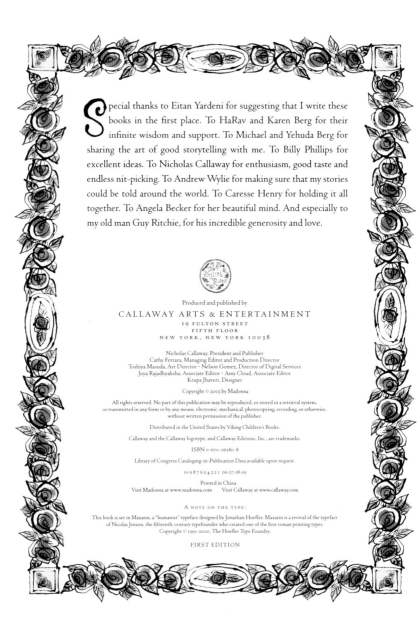

pecial thanks to Eitan Yardeni for suggesting that I write these books in the first place. To HaRav and Karen Berg for their infinite wisdom and support. To Michael and Yehuda Berg for sharing the art of good storytelling with me. To Billy Phillips for excellent ideas. To Nicholas Callaway for enthusiasm, good taste and endless nit-picking. To Andrew Wylie for making sure that my stories could be told around the world. To Caresse Henry for holding it all together. To Angela Becker for her beautiful mind. And especially to my old man Guy Ritchie, for his incredible generosity and love.

Produced and published by

CALLAWAY ARTS & ENTERTAINMENT

19 FULTON STREET
FIFTH FLOOR
NEW YORK, NEW YORK 10038

Nicholas Callaway, President and Publisher
Cathy Ferrara, Managing Editor and Production Director
Toshiya Masuda, Art Director · Nelson Gomez, Director of Digital Services
Joya Rajadhyaksha, Associate Editor · Amy Cloud, Associate Editor
Krupa Jhaveri, Designer

Distributed in the United States by Viking Children's Books.

Callaway and the Callaway logotype, and Callaway Editions, Inc., are trademarks.

ISBN 0-670-06180-8

Library of Congress Cataloging-in-Publication Data available upon request.

10 9 8 7 6 5 4 3 2 1 06 07 08 09

Printed in China
Visit Madonna at www.madonna.com   Visit Callaway at www.callaway.com

A NOTE ON THE TYPE:

This book is set in Mazarin, a "humanist" typeface designed by Jonathan Hoefler. Mazarin is a revival of the typeface
of Nicolas Jenson, the fifteenth-century typefounder who created one of the first roman printing types.
Copyright © 1991-2000, The Hoefler Type Foundry.

FIRST EDITION